Peter and the Wolf

The Five Mile Press Pty Ltd
1 Centre Road, Scoresby
Victoria 3179 Australia
www.fivemile.com.au

Part of the Bonnier Publishing Group
www.bonnierpublishing.com

First published 2015
Printed in China 5 4 3 2 1

Peter
and the
Wolf

Adapted and illustrated
by

Ayesha L. Rubio

The Five Mile Press

Early one morning, Peter opened his garden gate and walked out into the meadow.
There he met a bird singing cheerfully in the trees.

'Good morning, Peter,' said the bird as she jumped from one branch to another. 'What a peaceful morning!'

'It is peaceful,' thought Peter. There wasn't a gust of wind to ruffle the grass, or a trace of breeze to tickle the leaves.

The duck, who lived in Peter's backyard, swaggered down the path. Peter had left the garden gate open, so the duck decided to go for a swim in the pond near the meadow.

The bird flew from the tree and landed beside the pond.

'What kind of bird are you, if you can't fly?' she said to the duck.

'What kind of bird are you, if you can't swim?' answered the duck.

The bird and the duck argued for a while.

Suddenly, something caught Peter's attention.

Hidden by the tallest grass, a cat was watching them.

The cat thought he might be able to catch the bird while she was busy arguing with the duck.

The cat came closer. As he crept towards them, he started to imagine the bird between his claws.

'**Watch out!**' Peter shouted.

The bird flew straight to the highest branch of the tree.
With an offended quack, the duck swam quickly to the middle of the pond.

But the cat wasn't interested in the duck. He was walking in circles around the tree, wondering if he could reach the bird before she flew away.

Peter was so busy watching the bird and the cat that he didn't notice his grandpa arrive. Grandpa was very angry that Peter had wandered away from the garden.

'This is a dangerous place, Peter,' said Grandpa. 'What if a wolf from the forest came here? What would you do then?'

But Peter paid no attention to Grandpa's words.

'I'm not afraid of wolves,' he thought.

Grandpa took Peter home and locked the garden gate.

At that precise moment an enormous grey
wolf appeared from behind the trees.

The cat scurried up the tree and perched on the highest branch beside the bird.

The duck, who was very scared, hurried out of the pond. But she wasn't fast enough.

The wolf was getting closer and closer...
suddenly he opened his mouth and

swallowed the duck whole!

Peter watched in dismay from behind the garden gate. When he saw that Grandpa was distracted, he took a rope and rushed out into the meadow. He climbed up the tree and said to the bird,

'Fly over the wolf's head but be careful you don't get caught!'

While the bird distracted the wolf, Peter made a lasso with the rope.
He lowered it slowly until it fit perfectly around the wolf's tail.
Peter and the cat pulled with all their strength. The wolf was trapped.

But suddenly, from the shadow of the woods,
a band of hunters appeared.

They had been following the wolf's
tracks, and when they saw that the
wolf was caught,
they raised their guns.

'Don't shoot, please!' cried Peter.
'The bird, the cat and I have caught the wolf.
Let me make a deal with him.'

Peter carefully approached the wolf. He knelt down and whispered,
'Those hunters want either to kill you, or to trap you to sell in town.
I know it's been a hard winter and I know that you are hungry.
But that duck, who's still quacking in your belly, is my friend.

If you let her out I'll set you free. I promise.'

The wolf opened his mouth and spat the duck out from his belly.
The duck composed herself and started to scold the wolf with loud,
angry quacks. Peter set the wolf free, and the wolf ran quickly back
into the woods.

The hunters were very angry with Peter. But Grandpa managed
to calm them down.

So that is how Peter, the bird, the duck and the cat, became friends forever. They can often be found in the meadow or the woods, playing until dusk and running through the trees on the back of an enormous grey wolf.

The End

(No animals were harmed in the making of this book).